THE NOTEBOOK OF DOOM

RUMBLE OF THE COASTER GHOST

by Troy Cummings

BRANCHES

SCHOLASTIC INC.

TABLE OF CONTENTS

To the real-life Nikki, and all the scary students at Goolsby Elementary.

Thank you, Katie Carella and Liz Herzog. Working with you is like having the front seat on a 1,000-mile-long roller coaster. An absolute, nonstop, dizzying thrill!

Copyright © 2016 by Troy Cummings

All rights reserved. Published by Scholastic Inc., *Publishers since 1920.* SCHOLASTIC, BRANCHES, and associated logos are trademarks and/or registered trademarks of Scholastic Inc.

The publisher does not have any control over and does not assume any responsibility for author or third-party websites or their content.

No part of this publication may be reproduced, stored in a retrieval system, or transmitted in any form or by any means, electronic, mechanical, photocopying, recording, or otherwise, without written permission of the publisher. For information regarding permission, write to Scholastic Inc., Attention: Permissions Department, 557 Broadway, New York, NY 10012.

This book is a work of fiction. Names, characters, places, and incidents are either the product of the author's imagination or are used fictitiously, and any resemblance to actual persons, living or dead, business establishments, events, or locales is entirely coincidental.

Library of Congress Cataloging-in-Publication Data

Cummings, Troy, author.
Rumble of the coaster ghost / by Troy Cummings. – First edition.
pages cm. – (The Notebook of Doom ; 9)
Summary: Alexander's class is going on a field trip to an amusement park called Safety Land with really slow, boring rides–but this is Stermont, and when a weird magician tells Alexander and his friends that the roller coaster is haunted things start to get a lot more interesting.
ISBN 978-0-545-86497-8 (pbk.) – ISBN 978-0-545-86498-5 (hardcover)
1. Monsters–Juvenile fiction. 2. Roller coasters–Juvenile fiction. 3. Amusement parks–Juvenile fiction. 4. School field trips–Juvenile fiction. 5. Elementary schools–Juvenile fiction. 6. Friendship–Juvenile fiction. [1. Monsters–Fiction. 2. Roller coasters–Fiction. 3. Amusement parks–Fiction. 4. School field trips–Fiction. 5. Schools–Fiction. 6. Friendship–Fiction.] I. Title. II. Series: Cummings, Troy. Notebook of doom ; 9.
PZ7.C91494Ru 2016
813.6–dc23
[Fic]
2015020701

ISBN 978-0-545-86498-5 (hardcover) / ISBN 978-0-545-86497-8 (paperback)

10 9 8 7 6 5 4 3 2 1   16 17 18 19 20

Printed in China   38
First edition, February 2016

Book design by Liz Herzog

CHAPTER 1

THE NEW GIRL

Alexander Bopp was an expert at two things: fighting monsters and passing SUPER-SECRET notes in class. And today, he was passing a note *about* monster-fighting.

R+N:
Any signs of
FRUITCAKE
lately?

1

Alexander glanced at his teacher, Dr. Tallow. She was writing on the board. He passed the note back to his two best friends, Rip and Nikki. They sat in the back row.

Dr. Tallow turned around just as the note reached Nikki.

Nikki sank into her hoodie.

"Nikki, dearie," she said with an extra-wide smile. "Bring me the note, please."

Yikes, thought Alexander. *I'm glad I wrote* FRUITCAKE *instead of* MONSTERS.

"It would be a shame for you to miss out on our surprise field trip tomorrow, Nikki," Dr. Tallow continued. "Please bring me that note."

"Yeah, Nikki!" said Rip, sitting up straight. "Be a good student, like me!"

Nikki shot Rip a look. Then she handed the note to Dr. Tallow.

"All right, class," said Dr. Tallow, pocketing the note. "Now about that surprise! Tomorrow, we'll be taking a field trip to . . . an amusement park!"

The students cheered.

"Woohoohooo!" Rip howled. "An amusement park? On a school day?!"

KNOCK-KNOCK!

A serious-looking woman in a serious-looking suit was at the door. It was the school principal, Ms. Vanderpants.

"Dr. Tallow, I'm here with your new student," she said. "She'll start school tomorrow."

A shy-looking girl stepped into the room.

Dottie Rogers

Bunny shirt

Bunny socks

Bunny shoes

Bunny backpack

Alexander looked back at Rip and Nikki, who were grinning. They had all met Dottie at summer camp.

"Welcome to Stermont Elementary, Dottie," said Dr. Tallow. "We're glad to have you."

Alexander remembered his very first day at school. His teacher had called him "Salamander," which had become his nickname.

"Hi, Dottie!" said Alexander.

Dottie gave Alexander a little wave.

BRRIINNGGG!!

"Okay, dearies," said Dr. Tallow. "Give me your permission slips on the way out."

Alexander handed in his slip.

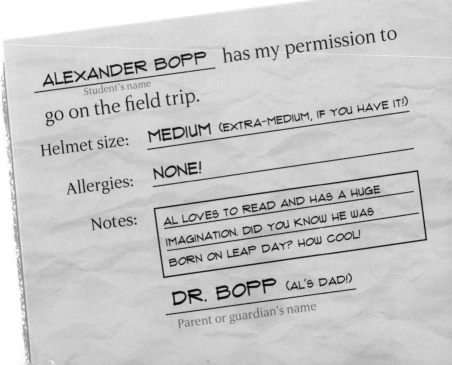

ALEXANDER BOPP has my permission to
Student's name
go on the field trip.

Helmet size: MEDIUM (EXTRA-MEDIUM, IF YOU HAVE IT!)

Allergies: NONE!

Notes: AL LOVES TO READ AND HAS A HUGE IMAGINATION. DID YOU KNOW HE WAS BORN ON LEAP DAY? HOW COOL!

DR. BOPP (AL'S DAD!)
Parent or guardian's name

CHAPTER 2 SOUP'S ON!

Alexander, Rip, and Nikki took the long way home. They followed a path through the woods that led to an old caboose, with the letters S.S.M.P. on the side.

SUPER SECRET MONSTER PATROL
CLUB MEMBERS

Alexander

The trusty leader!

Nikki

Brave and smart!

Rip

Loud and strong!
(But mostly loud.)

The three friends stepped inside S.S.M.P. headquarters. A map of Stermont hung on one wall, near a shelf full of random objects.

"I'm glad we stopped here," said Alexander. He loaded his backpack with monster-fighting gear.

Sharp pencil

Yo-yo

Flashlight

Potato-masher

Blindfold

Paperweight

Salt-shaker

Rubber gloves

"Don't forget the notebook," said Rip.

"Already in here," said Alexander. "I never go anywhere without it."

He pulled a beat-up notebook from inside the backpack.

S.S.M.P. =
(Super Secret Monster Patrol!)

CREEPY SKULL!

Full of monster drawings!

S.S.M.P.

DOOM!

"Now we'll be ready to fight all kinds of monsters," Alexander said.

Nikki coughed. "You mean *bad* monsters, right?" she said.

"Of course," said Alexander.

Nikki was actually a *good* monster, called a jampire.

JAMPIRES

LIKE: seeing in the dark, eating anything red and juicy.

DISLIKE: sunlight.

"You know," said Rip, putting his feet on the table, "Dr. Tallow is an awesome teacher. Her classroom-pet zone is super-fun, and now she's letting us ride *roller coasters*!"

"Yeah, whatever," Nikki said. "I think she's kind of—"

Nikki was interrupted by a voice shouting across the woods.

AL! DINNERTIME!

"Gotta go!" said Alexander, scooping up his backpack. "See you tomorrow!"

Alexander ran through the woods to his house.

His dad set two steaming bowls of tomato soup on the table.

"Dig in, Al!" he said. "I'll grab some drinks."

While his dad was in the kitchen, Alexander snuck a peek in the notebook. He was so focused on reading it that he missed his mouth with the spoon. **SPLAAARP!** Soup splattered everywhere.

I have to be more careful, he thought. *This notebook is the S.S.M.P.'s secret weapon!*

Alexander wiped the pages with his napkin.

BUMBLE-BEAVER
Busy, busy monster.

HABITAT Old, hollow logs.

TIMBERRRR!

Bumble-beavers build dams that are 100 feet tall.

DIET Twigs dipped in honey.

BEHAVIOR These creatures buzz around the forest, smelling flowers and knocking down trees.

WARNING! Even if you dodge the bumble-beaver's stinger, you could still get slapped by its tail!

THE SQUEALS ON THE BUS

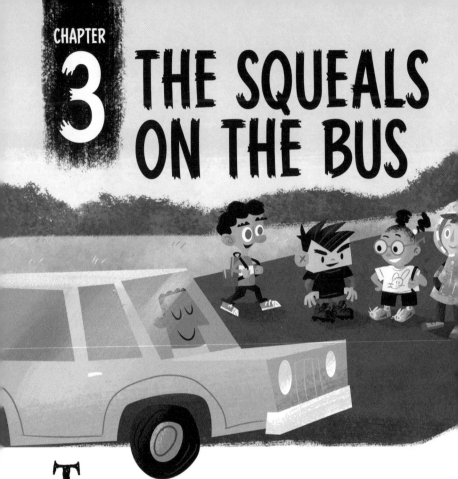

The next morning, Alexander's dad dropped Alexander off in the school parking lot.

The students were lining up near a bus. Rip and Nikki were already there, talking to Dottie.

"Hey, Salamander!" said Nikki. "We were just telling Dottie about our new school building."

"It's so fancy!" said Dottie.

"You're lucky, Dottie," said Nikki. "We used to go to school in an old hospital."

"You're double-lucky," Alexander added. "You get a field trip on your first day!"

Dottie smiled.

"You're triple-lucky . . ." said Rip, ". . . that you're allowed to board the bus with that goofy-looking backpack—OW!"

15

Nikki had pinched Rip's arm. "Ignore him, Dottie," she said. "We're glad you're here! Oh, look!" She pointed to a tall, white-haired man carrying a big cooler. "There's Mr. Hoarsely."

"Hoarsely's a huge weenie," said Rip. "He's afraid of everything,"

"Is he the bus driver?" asked Dottie.

"Yep," said Alexander. "He's also the school secretary, nurse, gym teacher, *and* janitor."

Alexander didn't mention that Mr. Hoarsely was a former member of the S.S.M.P. Or that he seemed to be the only grown-up who could see monsters.

"Morning, children!" said Mr. Hoarsely. He whistled as he boarded the bus.

"*Whoa!*" said Nikki. "Mr. Hoarsely looks so *calm* today!"

"And *happy!*" said Alexander.

Mr. Hoarsely stuck his head out the door. "All aboard!" he said. "The park opens in ten minutes!"

The students climbed onto the bus.

Dr. Tallow sat in the second row, digging through her purse.

Rip plopped down in the very first seat. "Let's sit up front with Dr. Tallow, guys!" he said.

"Well, good morning, Rip," said Dr. Tallow. "And hello, Alexander and Dottie!" She rubbed some lotion on her hands. "My skin gets so dry on warm days. Oh. Hello, Nikki."

Alexander, Rip, and Dottie smiled back. Nikki gave a silent nod.

Mr. Hoarsely started the engine. "We're off!" he yelled, as he drove out of the parking lot.

Rip leaned forward. "So does this amusement park have lots of cool rides?" he shouted to Mr. Hoarsely.

"You bet!" said Mr. Hoarsely. "They have a carousel, a haunted house, a roller coaster—you name it!"

"Yahoo!" Rip yelled. For the rest of the ride, he bounced in his seat.

At last, the bus came to a stop.

"Here we are!" Mr. Hoarsely said.

PSSSHT! The door slid open.

Rip shoved past Alexander and flew down the steps. **BLOMP!** He crashed right into a ten-foot-tall orange creature with a pointy head, white stripes, and huge, bulging eyes.

4 SAFETY LAND

MONSTER!" shouted Rip. "ATTACK!" He punched the creature in what he guessed was its gut.

"Oof!" said the big orange creature.

"Rip, stop!" cried Mr. Hoarsely, pulling Rip back. Everyone else climbed off the bus.

"Uh, Rip," said Alexander. "That's no monster."

Rip blinked. "It's not?"

Mr. Hoarsely turned to the students. "Meet Joan the Safety Cone! She's the mascot of this amusement park!"

"Fiddly-ho, boys and girls!" said the googly-eyed cone. "Welcome to Safety Land!"

Rip blinked again. "Wait. Did you say *safety*?"

"Yup!" said Joan.

"No wonder Mr. Hoarsely couldn't wait to come here," Alexander whispered to Rip and Nikki. "It's the safest place on Earth."

The grinning cone wheeled out a cart full of safety gear. "Everyone, put on your helmets!"

Dr. Tallow helped pass them out.

Alexander clipped on a helmet. Then he walked over to a big map. Nikki and Rip joined him. "Check it out," he said.

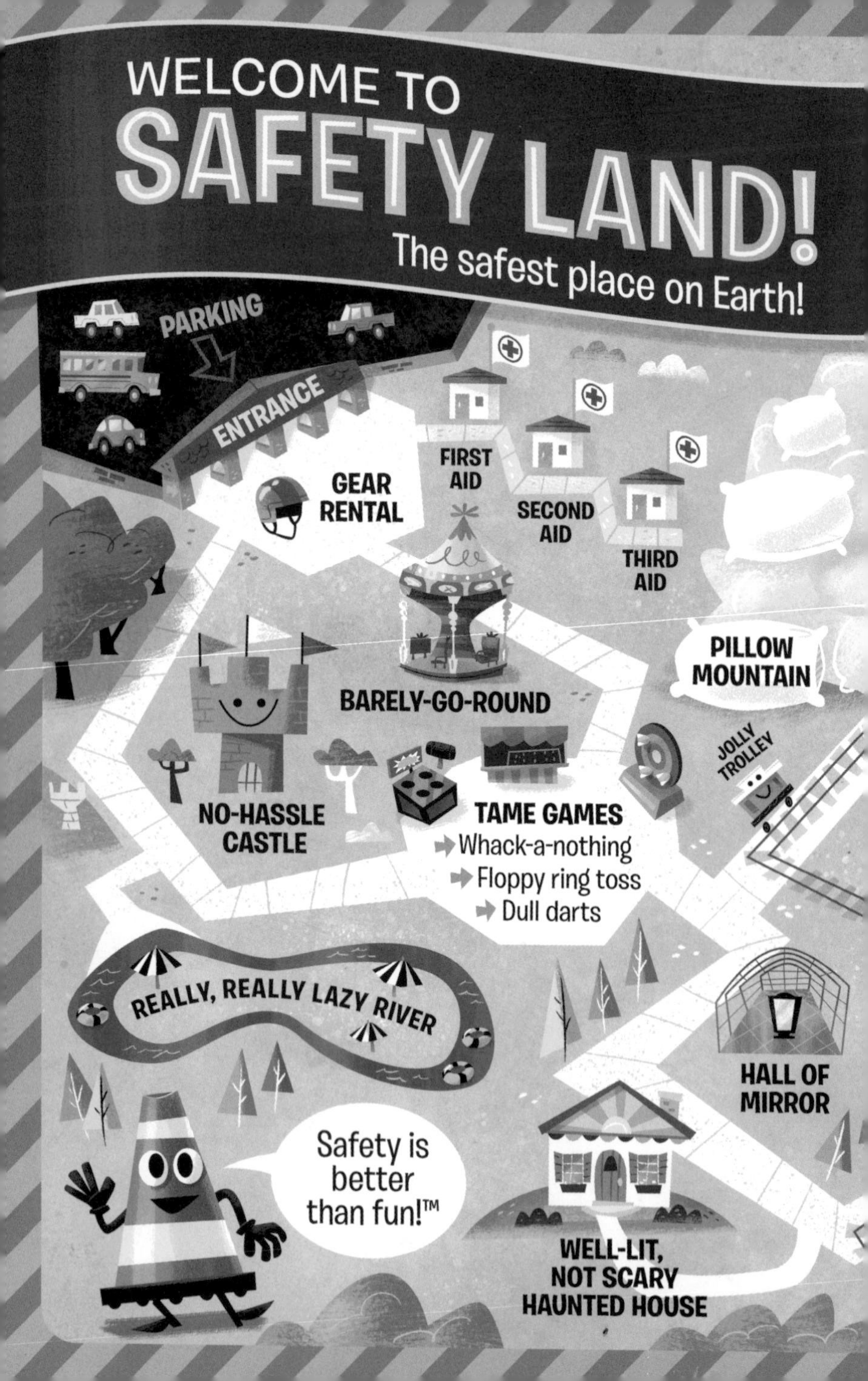

WELCOME TO
SAFETY LAND!
The safest place on Earth!

PARKING

ENTRANCE

GEAR RENTAL

FIRST AID

SECOND AID

THIRD AID

PILLOW MOUNTAIN

BARELY-GO-ROUND

JOLLY TROLLEY

NO-HASSLE CASTLE

TAME GAMES
→ Whack-a-nothing
→ Floppy ring toss
→ Dull darts

REALLY, REALLY LAZY RIVER

HALL OF MIRROR

Safety is better than fun!™

WELL-LIT, NOT SCARY HAUNTED HOUSE

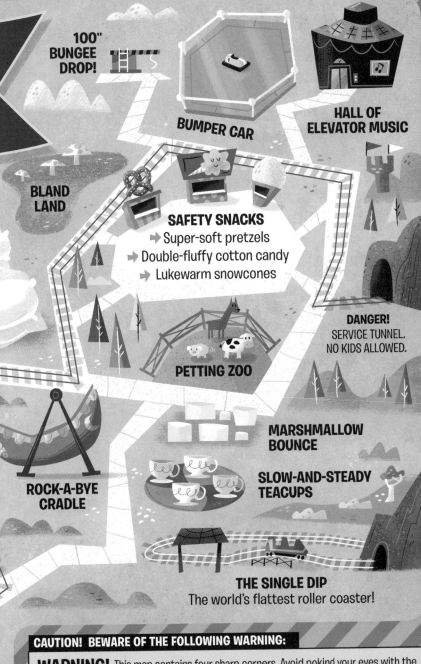

100" BUNGEE DROP!

BUMPER CAR

HALL OF ELEVATOR MUSIC

BLAND LAND

SAFETY SNACKS
➡ Super-soft pretzels
➡ Double-fluffy cotton candy
➡ Lukewarm snowcones

DANGER!
SERVICE TUNNEL.
NO KIDS ALLOWED.

PETTING ZOO

MARSHMALLOW BOUNCE

SLOW-AND-STEADY TEACUPS

ROCK-A-BYE CRADLE

THE SINGLE DIP
The world's flattest roller coaster!

CAUTION! BEWARE OF THE FOLLOWING WARNING:

WARNING! This map contains four sharp corners. Avoid poking your eyes with the edges of this map as you lean in to read the tiny, tiny words in this warning message.

"Hold on a sec," said Rip. "Slow teacups? A giant cradle? Is *everything* in this park safe?"

"You bet!" said Joan, skipping up behind them. "It's safety first! And second! And third! And—oops!" The top of the mascot costume fell off. The woman inside looked tired and sweaty.

"Crud!" she said. "The straps on this thing keep slipping. It's like they've been cut or something." She waved to Mr. Hoarsely. "Sir? Could you give me a hand?"

"Of course!" said Mr. Hoarsely, running over. In addition to his helmet, he wore elbow pads, knee pads, and a safety vest.

Rip turned back to the map. "Wait!" he said. "How about this roller coaster? That *must* be a real ride!"

"Huh?" said the woman, picking up her head. "Oh, sorry. The coaster is out of order. We had some . . . track damage."

Rip's eyes twitched. His fists shook. His face turned red. "Safety Land is the WORST!" he screeched.

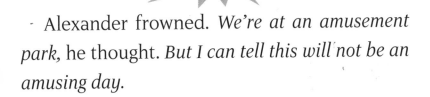

Alexander frowned. *We're at an amusement park,* he thought. *But I can tell this will not be an amusing day.*

CHAPTER 5 DOWN FOR THE COUNT

Fiddly-ho! Follow me, kids!"
Joan the Safety Cone led
Alexander's class on a parade
through the park.

Alexander noticed that everything in
Safety Land was soft. The handrails were
soft. The pretzels were soft. The sidewalks
were soft. Soft music even played in the
background.

At one point, Mr. Hoarsely sang along.

Gophers have holes.
Goldfish have bowls.

A hamburger hides in a bun.

Life can be swell
if you stay in your shell

**'CAUSE SAFETY IS
BETTER THAN FUN!**

"Here we are!" said Joan. "The world's safest haunted house!"

The parade stopped at a cozy cottage. There were no spiderwebs, no gravestones, and no old boarded-up windows.

"I'll lead the way!" yelled Mr. Hoarsely, adjusting his elbow pads.

Well-Lit, Not Scary
Haunted House

The door opened without making a creak, and Alexander's class walked inside. The room was well-lit, with thick carpeting, padded walls, and clearly marked emergency exits.

Alexander walked between Rip and Nikki. "Not exactly spooky, is it?" he said.

"Look!" said Mr. Hoarsely, clapping. "Magic!"

He pointed to a purple curtain covered with strange symbols.

"TA-DAAA!" An oddly dressed man stepped through the curtain.

He wore a wizard's hat, a tuxedo, and a shiny purple cape. His left arm was in a huge sling.

FLOMP! The curtain fell on the man's head.

"Oops, sorry!" he said. "Cheap curtain!" He tossed the curtain aside. Alexander noticed a zigzag cut along one edge.

"*Ahem,*" said the man. "I am the Wonderful, Mysterious, Amazing Count Chad!" He took a little bow. Half a deck of cards fell out of his sleeve.

The students giggled.

"No laughing!" snapped Count Chad. "I'm not a jokey magician—I'm a *real* magician!"

He wiped his brow, but his handkerchief was tied to four more handkerchiefs. They all became twisted in his sling.

"Now," Count Chad said, untangling himself, "watch me pull a rabbit from my hat!"

"*Oooh!*" said Dottie, smiling.

The magician reached into his hat and pulled out a half-eaten carrot. "*Hmmmmm,*" he said. "Maybe later."

"Oh," said Dottie, frowning.

"Instead, I WILL PREDICT THE FUTURE!" He wiggled his eyebrows as he pulled a crystal ball from his cape.

The ball began to glow.

Count Chad held the ball close to Alexander as he spoke. "I see a boy! A boy who has faced terrible, difficult, *monstrous* challenges!"

Alexander looked into the ball. Cloudy shapes danced in the glass.

"But this boy should beware . . ." continued Count Chad, ". . . of the dreadful, horrible, unspeakable COASTER GHOST!"

FLASH! The image in the crystal ball came into focus. Everyone gasped. A skull face with bloodshot eyes stared back at Alexander.

6 TEA FOR TWO

Alexander reached out to touch the crystal ball. The spooky eyes followed his finger.

"Hands off!" said Count Chad. He jerked his arm away. Alexander noticed an electric cord running from the bottom of the crystal ball. He looked at Nikki and raised an eyebrow.

"What's that?" asked Nikki, pointing.

"Uh . . . nothing!" said Count Chad. He took a step back and tripped over the cord.

WHOMP! He fell to the floor, and the crystal ball fell with him. The ball rolled to a stop on the carpet, completely dark.

"An *electric* crystal ball?" said Nikki.

"Totally lame!" said Rip.

Alexander could see that the ball was fake. But he could not stop thinking about those creepy eyes.

"Clumsy me!" said Count Chad, getting to his feet. "Now you know how I ended up with *this*!" He flapped his sling like a chicken wing.

Dr. Tallow shook her head. "That's enough magic for one day," she said. "Everyone pair up with a park-buddy on the way out."

Joan the Safety Cone waved the students toward the exit.

Dr. Tallow walked right over to Rip. "Dearie," she said. "I'd like you to be my park-buddy for the day."

"Sure!" said Rip. "Let's try that 100-foot bungee."

"I love bungee jumps!" said Dr. Tallow. "Really, anything stretchy."

"I'm going to the petting zoo," said Mr. Hoarsely. "Who's with me?"

"Me! Me!" said Dottie. "Maybe there are bunnies!"

100" Bungee →

Single Dip →

Petting Zoo →

Teacups →

Pillow Mountain ↑

Bland Land ↗

Alexander gave Nikki a smile. "Come on, park-buddy," he said. "Let's go ride something."

"Sure, Salamander," she said.

"Have fun, everyone!" yelled Dr. Tallow. "We'll meet at Pillow Mountain for lunch."

Alexander and Nikki wandered around the park.

Marshmallow Bounce

Rock-a-bye Cradle

Slow-and-steady Teacups

"At least there are no lines," said Alexander.

They ended up at the teacup ride. Alexander and Nikki plopped down in a yellow teacup.

Alexander grabbed the little chain to latch the teacup closed. "Hey, look," he said. "This chain's been snipped."

"I bet that's the most dangerous thing in Safety Land," Nikki said, rolling her eyes.

VWIRRRRRRR. The teacups started to spin, slowly.

"Wait," said Alexander. "The straps on Joan's costume and Count Chad's curtain had also been cut." He opened the notebook. "I remember reading about a scissor-monster in here . . ."

CUTTERFLY

Scissor-headed creature with paper wings

HABITAT Recycling bins.

DIET Coupons, paper-dolls, homemade valentines.

FUN FACT! Baby cutterflies look like safety scissors.

Nikki grabbed the notebook and snapped it shut. "No way, Salamander," she said. "A few snipped things don't equal a monster!"

Their teacup circled about, slow and steady.

"You know, Salamander, I don't think Dr. Tallow likes me," said Nikki.

"Really?" said Alexander. "Maybe she was upset about the note-passing, but—"

"Hey! Weenies!" shouted Rip.

CLUNK. The teacup came to a stop.

Rip ran up to them, with Dr. Tallow lagging behind. "It turns out that ride was a 100-*inch* bungee! Basically one big rubber band."

"Or maybe it *used to be* a 100-foot bungee," said Alexander, thinking out loud, "and it got snipped—by a monster!"

"Huh?" said Rip. "No! Everything here is just super safe!"

Maybe not everything, thought Alexander. He checked the sky for fluttering cutterflies, but the only thing fluttering was his stomach.

CHAPTER 7 FLIPPED LID

At lunchtime, the students gathered near Pillow Mountain.

Dr. Tallow counted heads, and recounted heads. She frowned.

"*Hmm . . .*" she said. "Everyone's here but Mr. Hoarsely and Dottie."

"Maybe Count Chad made them disappear," said Rip, in a fake-spooky voice.

Dr. Tallow chuckled. "Well, I'm sure they'll be here soon. Let's start eating."

She turned to Nikki. "Sweetie, could you pass out the lunches? They're in the cooler."

"Uh, okay," said Nikki. She walked over to pick up the cooler.

KERPLOF! The lid snapped in half.

Dr. Tallow scowled. "What did you do?"

"I—I don't know!" Nikki said. "The lid was just—sliced down the middle!"

Alexander's eyes widened.

"All right, Nikki," said Dr. Tallow. "Have a seat."

Nikki grumbled as she sat between Rip and Alexander.

Dr. Tallow passed out the lunches. There were mini-menus stapled to the bags.

Rip chomped a corn chip.

"I don't have super-strength," said Nikki, wadding up her paper bag. "That cooler was already broken!"

"Just like Joan's costume," added Alexander, "and Count Chad's curtain. And the teacup chain!"

"I don't know about that," said Rip. "I think you're starting to imagine monsters because this a-*snooze*-ment park is booooring."

"It's too bad the roller coaster is busted," said Nikki.

Alexander sipped his juice. "Wait a minute," he said. "Maybe a *ghost* broke the coaster! Didn't the crystal ball warn us about a *coaster* ghost?"

"Ha!" said Nikki. "You mean the *fake* crystal ball?"

"Good point," said Alexander. "But still, I saw spooky eyes in the ball."

"Oh geez, Salamander!" Rip snorted. "First, monsters. Now, *ghosts*? You're a bigger weenie than Hoarsely today!"

Alexander stuck out his blue tongue at Rip. But he kept thinking about those eyes. *They seemed so real—almost like I've seen them before . . .*

HIDE-AND GO-*EEP!*

After lunch, Alexander's classmates lined up for the Barely-go-round.

"Should we give it a go?" Alexander asked Rip and Nikki.

BARELY-GO-ROUND

NO UP-AND-DOWN HORSES!

SEAT BELTS!

AIR BAGS!

SNAIL-SPEED!

"Forget that baby ride!" said Rip. "Let's play ring toss!"

Alexander and Nikki followed Rip to a game booth. Joan the Safety Cone stood behind the counter.

Rip paid a dollar for a floppy ring.

He tossed the ring. **PLINK!** It landed on a peg.

"Fiddly-ho! Way to go!" said Joan.

"So what's my prize?" asked Rip.

"You get to keep the ring!" said Joan. She tossed the ring back to Rip.

Rip frowned. "I paid a whole dollar for *this*?" Alexander and Nikki laughed as Rip slipped the ring on his wrist.

"Excuse me." Dr. Tallow stepped in front of Nikki. She leaned down to talk to Alexander and Rip. "You two are such responsible students. Could you do me a favor?"

"Sure!" said Rip.

Alexander saw Nikki grit her teeth.

Dr. Tallow lowered her voice. "Dottie and Mr. Hoarsely are still not back yet. Could you run a loop around the park to look for them?"

"Uh, Nikki's my park-buddy," said Alexander. "Can she come with us?"

Dr. Tallow paused. "Of course, dearie," she said.

"Okay guys, let's go!" said Alexander. "We'll hit the petting zoo first!"

The friends ran past rides, game booths, and snack carts.

They finally arrived at the petting zoo: a fake ranch filled with giant stuffed animals.

"I should've known!" said Nikki. "*Real* animals would be too dangerous for Safety Land."

Rip tried to pet a cow, but it tipped over.

"Sheesh!" he said. He unsnapped his helmet and strapped it to the cow's head. "You need this more than I do."

"*Eep!*" shouted a giant stuffed llama.

Actually, it wasn't a giant stuffed llama. It was a tall person crouched down behind a llama.

"Mr. Hoarsely!" said Nikki. "Where have you been?"

"I've been hiding!" said Mr. Hoarsely. His kneepads made a *clack-clack-clack* sound as they knocked together. "Count Chad was right. The coaster ghost is real!"

"Where's Dottie?" asked Rip.

"I think the ghost got her!" cried Mr. Hoarsely. "We were near the roller coaster when we heard a terrible noise. Then I ran!"

"You left Dottie all alone?" asked Alexander.

GGGRUUUUMMMM!! A thunderous rumble rang out across the park.

Mr. Hoarsely jumped into the pouch of a giant kangaroo.

"Mr. Hoarsely," said Alexander, "head back to Pillow Mountain! We'll find Dottie!"

Mr. Hoarsely hopped the fence and ran.

Alexander, Rip, and Nikki ran the other way. Toward the roller coaster.

CHAPTER 9 SINGLE DIP

WARNING!

The Single Dip
CONTROL BOOTH

OUT OF ORDER

They call *that* a roller coaster?" yelled Rip, shaking his head.

There was a sign lying on the ground. Nikki picked it up.

"Look, guys!" she said. "This rope has been snipped!"

OUT OF ORDER

"See, Rip?" said Alexander. "Somebody has been cutting stuff all over the park!"

"Okay, fine, Salamander," said Rip. "But so what?! And why cut *that* rope? The ride is out of order with or without the sign!"

Just then, an empty roller coaster car rolled into view, and stopped.

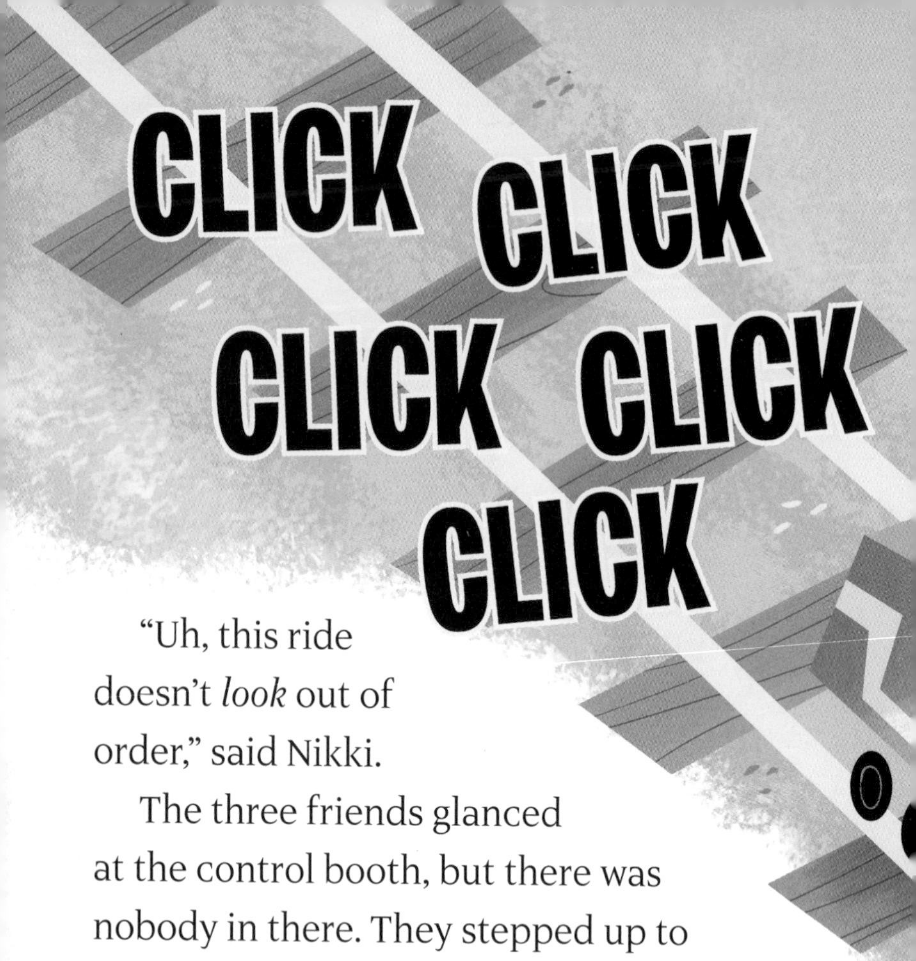

**CLICK CLICK
CLICK CLICK
CLICK**

"Uh, this ride doesn't *look* out of order," said Nikki.

The three friends glanced at the control booth, but there was nobody in there. They stepped up to the coaster.

"Look! What's that in the front seat?" said Rip.

"Something fuzzy," said Nikki. "And rabbity!"

"Dottie's backpack!" cried Alexander.

"How did it get here?" asked Nikki.

"Beats me," said Rip, scratching his head. "But there's no way a *ghost* put it here."

"Not a ghost …" said Alexander. "That's it! Those eyes in the crystal ball! They weren't *ghost* eyes—they belong to a whirly-wisp!"

He opened the notebook.

The Single Dip
CONTROL BOOTH

WHIRLY-WISP

Looks like a ghost, but it's not.
(There's no such thing as ghosts.)

Skull head

Glowing red eyes

Raggedy body

Dark caves.

GRUMMM!

A whirly-wisp's growl sounds like a rumbling train.

DIET > Jellied kid brains (served on crackers).

BEHAVIOR > The whirly-wisp turns anything it touches to jelly.

WARNING!

This monster will stop at nothing to eat your brains! But if you can draw a circle around it, the whirly-wisp will fade away.

"Those eyes *do* look similar . . ." said Nikki.

"And we do keep hearing a rumbling sound," added Alexander.

"So let's wallop this whirly-wisp!" said Rip. "Before it turns Dottie into jelly!"

BRUGHMMMMMMMM! A rumble blasted from the tunnel.

"Come on! The coaster is about to move," said Alexander. He hopped into the car. Rip and Nikki got into the seat behind him.

PSSHHHHT! The coaster carried them down a hill, over a bump, and into the tunnel. Right toward the terrible sound.

10 TUNNEL VISION

Rip held up his arms, ready to say *weeeee!* as the coaster rolled into the tunnel.

But he didn't say *weeeeeee*. He didn't even say *woo*. He just made a sound like a balloon losing air.

"That was some dip," Rip said. "I've ridden shopping carts faster than this!"

SPEED LIMIT 2

SAFETY FIRST

Alexander looked around. The tunnel walls were painted to look like a cave, with fake, rubbery rocks all around.

Suddenly—**CLACK!** The coaster came to a stop.

"What happened?" asked Nikki.

SHUFF. SHUFF. There was a sound like footsteps up ahead.

"Did you hear that?" Alexander whispered. He craned his neck to see around the bend. A second track branched off to the left, but the footsteps seemed to be coming from another direction.

CLONK! The lights went out.

"*Whoa!*" said Rip.

The three friends leaned in close to one another.

SHUFF. SHUFF. SHUFF. The footsteps were coming closer.

"Nikki," whispered Alexander, "what can you see with your night-vision?"

"Someone's coming this way," whispered Nikki. She gasped, then shouted: "Dottie!"

"Hey!" Dottie called back. "Who turned out the lights?"

Alexander unzipped his backpack. "Hang on, Dottie!" he shouted. "I've got a flashlight!" He flicked it on.

Dottie ran over to the coaster.

"What are you *doing* down here?" asked Rip.

"Well, Mr. Hoarsely ran off," said Dottie. "So I turned to head back for lunch. But then I saw a bunny by this ride! I tossed my backpack into a parked coaster car and chased the bunny down here. But I lost it after 99 hops!"

"See, Salamander?" Rip said. "There was never a ghost—or a monster!"

Alexander turned back to Dottie. "Did you see glowing red—"

BRUGHMMMMMMMMM! A deep rumble shook the tunnel. Alexander saw something move, just to his left. He swept his flashlight along the wall, and stopped when the light hit a creepy-looking rock.

Actually, it wasn't a rock. It was a floating body made of dark, twisted rags. A grinning skull bobbled on top of the body. The creature drifted toward the coaster car. Its red, glowing eyes lit up the tunnel.

"The whirly-wisp!" said Alexander.

"A*aaarrghhh!*" Rip, Nikki, and Alexander screamed as they leaped from the coaster. They landed near Dottie.

The creature opened its jaws.

BRUGGGHHHHHHHHHHMM

Its howl shook the tunnel.

"The ghost!" said Dottie. "It's real!"

"It's not a ghost," said Nikki. "It's a whirly-wisp!"

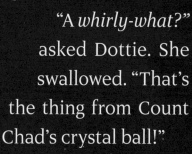

!MMMM!!

"A *whirly-what?*" asked Dottie. She swallowed. "That's the thing from Count Chad's crystal ball!"

The creature floated toward Alexander, its head bobbing.

"Don't be scared, Dottie," said Rip. "We're professionals."

Alexander took a step away from his friends. The creature lurched at him.

"Watch out, Salamander!" said Rip. "Don't let it touch you!"

BRUGGGHHMMM!!! The skull head began to spin around.

"What's happening?!" asked Dottie.

Alexander pulled a pencil from his backpack. "If the whirly-wisp tags me, I'll turn to jelly. But if I'm fast enough—"

With low, quick steps, he ran a loop around the creature. He dragged his pencil along the ground, drawing a circle.

"That should do it!" said Nikki. "So long, whirly-wisp!"

The creature twisted and jerked.

"Didn't the notebook say the monster was supposed to disappear as soon as the circle was drawn?!" yelled Rip.

The creature flopped in place, still making a rumbling sound.

"Wait a second," said Alexander. He reached up to grab the edge of the creature's gown.

"Salamander, no!" Nikki yelled.

12 ALL TIED UP

FWOOF! Alexander yanked the sheet off the creature.

"Aha!" he said. "This whirly-wisp was a fake!"

String

Pulleys

Rubber skull

Lights

BRUGGGHHHH

Loudspeaker

Sliced-up sheet

67

"We've been tricked!" said Rip.

"But why?" asked Nikki.

"And who would do something like this?" added Dottie.

Alexander turned off the loudspeaker. The tunnel became quiet.

SHUFF. SHUFF. Alexander heard new footsteps. Alexander, Rip, Nikki, and Dottie all turned to see an oddly dressed man carrying a lantern. The man had one arm in a huge sling.

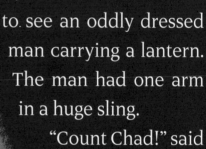

"Count Chad!" said Rip.

"Thank goodness you're here!" cried Dottie, smiling.

"How did you find us?" asked Nikki.

Count Chad tugged at his beard. "A good magician never reveals his tricks!"

"Can you get us out of here?" asked Dottie.

"*Hmmm . . .*" said Count Chad, stroking his beard. "I think I'd rather show you my latest trick."

"Huh?" said Rip.

FWISH! A lasso of colorful scarves shot from the magician's sleeve, binding Alexander's arms to his sides.

"*Oof!*" Alexander fell onto the tracks.

"Presto!" said Count Chad. "You've tumbled right into my trap!"

The magician smiled at Rip, Nikki, and Dottie. The friends took a few steps back.

"You three," he said, "will be the audience for my next magic trick!"

He raised his sling above his head.

69

CRACK! Count Chad's huge sling burst open, revealing a spiky crab claw.

"You're the one who's been cutting stuff up?!" said Nikki, wide-eyed.

"You got it!" said the crab creature.

SNIP-SNIP-SNIP! Count Chad's claw sliced off his cape. Then he yanked off his fake beard and tossed it aside.

"TA-DAAAAA!" he said. "I'm the wonderful, mysterious, amazing CRAB-RA CADABRA!"

Alexander squirmed. The monster leaned down to pat his head. "Alexander Bopp! I knew you'd follow my fake monster clues!"

Dottie gave Alexander a strange look. "This guy *knows* you?" she said.

"I—I don't know," said Alexander.

The crab creature laughed. "Every monster knows the Super Secret Monster Patrol!" he said. "We've been trying to stop the S.S.M.P. since forever! And finally: hocus-pocus! I've trapped the leader!"

Rip took a baby step toward Alexander.

CLICKA-CLICK! The creature pointed his claw at Alexander. "You! The boy tied up on the tracks! You'll help me with the old saw-the-boy-in-half trick!"

"What?! No!" cried Nikki.

"I could use my *claw* as the saw . . ." the monster continued, ". . . but cutting you in half with this roller coaster will be *way* more fun!"

The crab-ra cadabra scuttled over to a panel near the service tunnel. "It's show time!" he said. He pressed GO.

Rip rushed over to Alexander and began yanking on the scarves.

"Rip, hurry!" yelled Alexander. He could feel the rumble of the cold metal track as the coaster rolled closer.

13 DEAD END.

A lexander flopped around like a trout. But he couldn't get off the tracks. His arms were bound tight, and the coaster car was inching toward him.

"Run for it!" Alexander shouted to his friends.

"Not without you!" said Nikki. "Rip! Dottie! Let's lift him into the coaster!"

"This ought to be good," said the crab-ra cadabra, smiling. He propped himself up on a fake boulder to watch.

With a grunt, Rip, Nikki, and Dottie hoisted Alexander up to the edge of the moving car and—**OOF!**—dumped him in. Then they jumped in, too.

"So long, pincher-brain!" said Rip. "You'll never catch us now!"

The car coasted ahead at one mile per hour.

"BAR-HAR-HAR!" The monster laughed.

"Thanks for saving me!" said Alexander.

"Don't thank us yet," said Nikki. "We're not exactly making a speedy getaway."

The crab-ra cadabra scuttled past the car, over to the tunnel exit. Then he opened his claw above a piece of track. **CLANK!** He clamped down, snipping the metal like cardboard.

"Dead end!" said the monster.

The car inched forward.

"The big boss was totally right!" the monster continued. "She knew you'd stick together to save Alexander instead of running to safety."

"Wait," said Rip. "You have a *boss*?"

"Sure," said the crab-ra cadabra. "The boss-monster! She's in charge. And I'll show her I'm better than the balloon goons, the P-rex—all those dumb monsters!"

"Better at what?" asked Nikki.

"Better at crushing the S.S.M.P., once and for all," said the monster. "Finally, Stermont will belong to us!"

"Not a chance!" shouted Alexander. He wriggled around, trying to see where their car was headed. It was coasting straight for the broken tracks, where the giant crab stood grinning. His sharp claw sparkled in the lantern light.

CLICKA!
CLICKA!
CLICK!

14 ON THE WRONG TRACK

"**G**uys, untie me NOW!" shouted Alexander. His arms were numb from the tight scarves.

Nikki and Dottie reached over and began fiddling with the knots.

"It's tricky!" cried Nikki. "The scarves are all twisted!"

"Hurry up!" yelled Rip. "Before Count Crab Cake snips us *all* in half!"

Alexander watched the tunnel wall roll by. He could hear the **CLICKA-CLICK!** of the crab-monster's claw growing louder as they coasted toward the broken end of the track.

Then Alexander noticed the SERVICE TUNNEL switch.

"Rip!" he shouted. "Ring toss!"

"Huh?" said Rip. Alexander nodded to the switch.

"Oh!" Rip pulled the ring off his arm and flung it at the switch.

DING! The switch flipped.

KA-THUNK!

The tracks shifted.

The coaster veered left. **SNIP!**

The monster's massive claw lopped off the top of Rip's hair.

Rip ran a shaky hand across the top of his head. "Why'd I give my helmet to a cow?" he said.

The coaster rolled into the service tunnel.

"You're not getting away that easy!" said the crab-ra cadabra.

SLAM! The monster leaped onto the back of the car.

Suddenly, the track angled down. Straight down.

Alexander's stomach flipped. Everyone screamed as the coaster raced downward at rocket-speed.

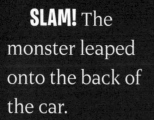

"Now *this* is a roller coaster!" Rip shouted.

The monster was holding on tight.

The coaster roared through the twisting underground passage and thundered around a corner.

"Look—daylight!" Dottie shouted. "We're headed outside!"

WHOOSH! The coaster blasted out of the tunnel and onto a set of trolley tracks.

The coaster sped along. Rides, game booths, and snack stands flew past in a colorful blur.

URGHHH! With a grunt, the crab-ra cadabra leaped over the coaster car. He landed on the track and tucked himself into his shell. The coaster barreled toward him.

"Hang on!" yelled Alexander.

CLANG! The coaster rammed into the monster's hard shell. The shell stayed put. But the coaster launched high into the sky.

CHAPTER 15 SECRET WEAPON

"A*AAAAAAAH!*" The heavy coaster car flew through the air, over the Rock-a-bye Cradle ride ... **PLOOOMP!** and bounced on a giant white cushion.

Alexander opened his eyes. His arms were still tied, but he was alive. "Hey—soft landing!" he said.

"I never thought I'd say this," Rip said. "But I'm glad we're at *Safety* Land."

Nikki looked around. "But where did the monster go?"

"I'm out of here!" said Dottie. She ran and hid behind a cotton-candy cart.

Rip pulled Alexander to his feet. "Let's finally get you untied, Salamander, before—"

Marshmallow Bounce

SCRITCHA-SCRITCHA-SCRITCH!!!

The crab creature skittered into view. "All right kids—chop-chop!" he said.

"Run!" said Nikki.

The S.S.M.P. ran to the nearest ride—the teacups. Rip and Nikki dove into a pink teacup, and Alexander flopped into a yellow one. They all ducked down to hide.

The crab-ra cadabra stepped onto the ride. His massive shell brushed against the ride's controls. The teacups began to spin around slowly.

"Oh, goodie!" the monster shouted. "A game!"

He swung his claw down hard . . .

. . . shattering a purple teacup.

"Nobody there!" said the crab-ra cadabra. "I'll try again!"

The monster smashed another teacup. There were just two left.

Alexander peeked over the brim of his cup. The monster held his claw high above Rip and Nikki's cup.

Alexander popped up and shouted, "Stop! Don't hurt them! Take me, but leave my friends alone."

"How about we make a deal?" asked the monster. "Hand over your secret weapon, and I'll let you *all* go."

"Secret weapon?" said Alexander.

The monster rolled his beady eyes. "You know! The *notebook!* The boss-monster wants me to bring it to her. Then the S.S.M.P. will no longer have the upper claw—I mean, hand."

Huh? The monsters know about the notebook?! thought Alexander.

"Hand it over NOW!" yelled the crab.

Alexander saw Rip and Nikki peeking out of their teacup. They shook their heads no. The crab-ra cadabra raised his claw higher.

Alexander wobbled out of his cup. "You win."

The monster lowered his claw. "Good move, kid," he said. "Now I'll cut your arms free so you can hand over the notebook."

SNIP! The claw shredded the scarves. Alexander shook the numbness from his arms. Then he opened his backpack, pulled out the notebook, and handed it to the monster.

16 GET CRACKIN'

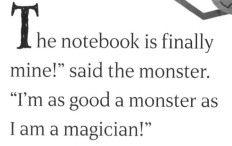

The notebook is finally mine!" said the monster. "I'm as good a monster as I am a magician!"

"Oh, please!" Nikki shouted from her teacup. "You're a terrible magician!"

The crab-ra cadabra's face became stop-sign red. "Oh yeah?" he said.

He tucked the notebook under his arm. Then he reached into his hat and pulled out a squirming bunny.

"Watch me make this rabbit disappear!" said the monster.

He held the bunny up. Then he opened his giant claw.

"NO!" shouted Dottie, popping up from her hiding spot. "Don't you *dare* hurt that bunny!"

She ran over to the teacup controls and slid the lever from SAFE to FUN.

The teacups began to spin. The notebook flew out from under the monster's arm. Alexander caught it, before falling on a pile of teacup parts. Rip and Nikki ducked down in their cup as the teacups spun faster and faster.

"Yikes!" cried the monster. He dropped the bunny and quickly tucked himself into his shell.

The cups rattled on their saucers.

WHOOP! The crab's shell spun like a top. It spun off the ride and down the sidewalk.

Dottie smiled as she turned off the ride. Alexander, Rip, and Nikki stumbled to the sidewalk, dizzy, but happy.

"That . . . was . . . awesome!" mumbled Rip, before falling over.

The crab was still spinning in his shell, like a confused break-dancer. He whirled across the sidewalk, through a flowerbed, and right into the path of the Rock-a-bye Cradle.

"Good job, Dottie!" said Alexander. "There's just one thing left to do!" He dashed over to the cradle's controls and hit GO.

KRUNNCCHHHH!!!

The huge cradle rocked forward, shattering the crab's hard shell. The pale, flabby monster shivered without his shell.

"*Noooo!!!!*" he groaned. "That shell was my armor—my home!"

"*Whoa!*" said Rip. "He's so . . . pale!"

"And so squishy!" said Nikki.

"And so not-at-all fluffy!" said Dottie.

SPLOOSH! The creature flopped into a sewer drain.

A moment later, Dr. Tallow ran into view, stepping over pieces of shattered teacups and crab shell.

"Alexander!" she said. "What happened?"

"Uh, we found Dottie," said Alexander.

"Oh . . . very good," said Dr. Tallow. She took Dottie's hand. "Come along, Dottie, let's get you some lunch."

Dottie looked back and waved to Alexander, Rip, and Nikki.

Alexander held a finger to his lips. *Shhh!*

Dottie gave Alexander a thumbs-up.

Alexander, Rip, and Nikki stayed behind.

"There's no way the crab-ra cadabra will find a shell *that* big again," said Rip.

"Yeah, we cracked this monster," said Nikki. "But what about the *boss-monster* he mentioned? Do you think there's one big monster in charge?"

Alexander frowned. "I don't know," he said. "But if monsters *are* after the notebook, we'll need to be more careful than ever."

"Speaking of *careful*," said Rip, "why don't we go ride the Barely-go-round?"

"Without your helmet?" asked Nikki.

Alexander laughed. "We'll get it back from the cow after I update the notebook."

CRAB-RA CADABRA

Crab monster with a few tricks
up its sleeve.

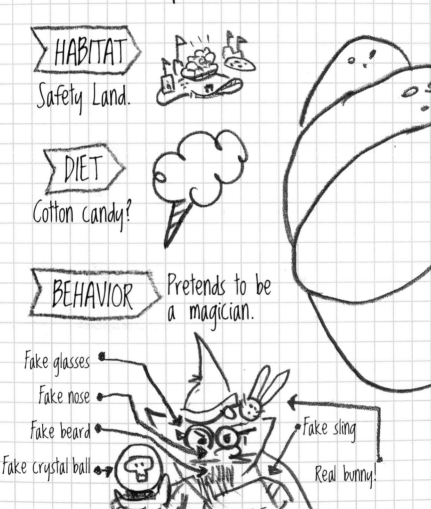

> **HABITAT**

Safety Land.

> **DIET**

Cotton candy?

> **BEHAVIOR** Pretends to be
a magician.

Fake glasses

Fake nose

Fake beard

Fake crystal ball

Fake sling

Real bunny!

CRACK! This monster is harmless without its shell.

WARNING! The crab-ra cadabra's claw can snip through anything: ropes, chains, and roller coaster tracks.

TROY CUMMINGS

has no tail, no wings, no fangs, no claws, and only one head. As a kid, he believed that monsters might really exist. Today, he's sure of it.

BEHAVIOR This creature is scared to death of roller coasters, but rides them anyway.

HABITAT About a 20-minute bus ride from Safety Land.

DIET Crab cake sandwiches, with lots of lemon.

EVIDENCE Few people believe that Troy Cummings is real. The only proof we have is that he supposedly wrote and illustrated The Eensy-Weensy Spider Freaks Out!, and Giddy-up, Daddy!

WARNING Keep your eyes peeled for more danger in The Notebook of Doom #10:

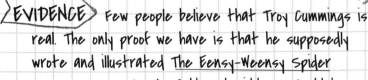

SNAP OF THE SUPER-GOOP

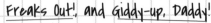

THE NOTEBOOK OF DOOM

QUESTIONS & ACTIVITIES!

How is the amusement park **different** than what Rip expected?

How does the S.S.M.P. know the monster is not a cutterfly or a whiry-whisp?

New girl to the rescue! How does Dottie save the day?

Who is the boss-monster? Write your opinion and explain your thoughts.

What is *your* favorite ride at the amusement park? Draw the ride and write why it is your favorite.